Enid and the Dangerous Discovery

By Cynthia G. Williams

Illustrated by Betty Harper

Published in 1999
by Broadman & Holman Publishers, Nashville, Tennessee

Printed in the United States of America
All rights reserved
ISBN 0-8054-1884-9
Art direction and design by Jennifer Davidson

The right of Cynthia G. Williams and Betty Harper to
be identified as the author and illustrator respectively
of this work has been asserted.

Scripture quotations are from the *King James Version*.

Library of Congress Cataloging-in-Publication Data

Williams, Cynthia G., 1958-
    Enid and the dangerous discovery / Cynthia G. Williams ;
    illustrated by Betty Harper.
        p.   cm. -- (Our neighborhood)
    ISBN 0-8054-1884-9
    [1. Firearms Ficton.   2. Afro-Americans Fiction.]   I. Harper,
    Betty, ill.   II. Title.   III. Series: Williams, Cynthia G., 1958-
    Our neighborhood.
    PZ7.W6559235Eo   1999
    [Fic] --dc21
                                                    99-27619
                                                    CIP

        1 2 3 4 5 03 02 01 00 99

BROADMAN
&HOLMAN
PUBLISHERS

I dedicate my first children's book to Mother, who calls
me her rose. I am, she says, the beautiful, God-given bloom
she carefully cultivates, thorns and all.
If I am her rose, then she is the one who grounds me
with unconditional love that allows my spirit to soar.

Cynthia G. Williams

*By this we know that we love the children of God,
when we love God, and keep his commandments.*
(I John 5: 2, KJV)

Grandma's old rocking chair made its familiar sound as Enid listened from the porch step below. The creaking rhythm sounded as familiar to her as a lullaby.

"Grandma," Enid asked, resting her face in her hand as she looked out toward the street. "What does it feel like to be shot?"

Suddenly the rocking chair's lullaby stopped, and Enid waited for an answer.

"Child, what kind of thing is that for a little girl to be wondering about?"

Enid looked up. Grandma's face had that odd expression, like the time she caught Enid stealing icing from a chocolate cake.

"Well, at school today, this boy in the seventh grade got sent home for pointing a play gun at another student."

"Good!" said Grandma, sitting back in her chair and starting to rock again. "Teachers can't tolerate even pretend guns at school these days. Back when I was a little girl growing up in the country, Papa would take his rifle out huntin' to put meat on the table for us to eat. But these days, folks seem to be huntin' one another. Times have just gotten too bad."

Frustrated that her question hadn't been answered, Enid stamped her foot and tried again. "But what does it feel like to be shot?"

"It's a feeling you never want to have or give to anybody else, Enid. Now go on and play. Your momma will be home soon and she wants you to be on time for choir rehearsal tonight."

Enid jumped down from the porch step and headed for her best friend's house. It wasn't long before she saw Violet, sitting cross-legged in her yard, drawing in the dirt with a stick.

Enid tiptoed up behind Vi and put both hands over her eyes.

"Enid, girl, I know that's you!"

"How did you know that?" Enid asked, disappointed that her surprise had failed.

"Well first of all, I saw you coming down the street. And second, you're the only friend I have who tries to surprise somebody by sneaking up on them all the time. After about the fifth time, Enid, it stopped being a surprise."

Vi went back to drawing in the dirt, pleased with herself.

"You're just making that up," Enid said. "Besides, I know a secret."

"Oh, you mean about that boy being put out of school for having a play gun?" Vi answered in the same sing-song voice.

"How did you find out?"

"Enid, everybody saw him playing with that plastic gun, so everybody knows."

Enid sat down beside her friend, and asked seriously, "I wonder what it feels like to get shot, Vi?"

"Girl, I don't ever wanna' know. My cousin got shot a long time ago. He was just cleaning his gun and it went off. He was in the hospital for a month!"

Enid was about to press Vi for more details when their friend Ron pulled up on his bicycle.

"Did you all hear about that play gun in school today?" he asked.

"Yeah, we know," both girls said, rolling their eyes in reply.

"Well, it's supposed to be on the news tonight. I saw the TV reporter at school getting pictures when they were taking the boy away."

W here did they take him?" Enid asked.

"Probably to jail," Ron replied.

"No they didn't!" Vi said. "They took him over to his aunt's house because they didn't know how to find his mom or dad. He'll probably be back in school next week."

"Well anyway, he's in a lot of trouble! I wouldn't want to be in his shoes," Ron piped up. "Say, I'm out of here."

"Where you going?" Enid asked.

"To look for Ment. Want to come?"

"No, I have choir practice at the church tonight, so I've got to be going in a while," Enid said.

"Check you later then," Ron called as he rode off on his bicycle.

Enid and Violet were playing jump rope when Enid suddenly remembered the promise to her mother about choir practice. "I have to go, Vi. It's getting dark, and I'll be in big trouble if I miss choir practice. I sure hope I'm not late."

"See you tomorrow," Vi called. "Hope you already got those math problems done."

Enid laughed at her friend. "Sure do," she called as she left the yard.

She was down the street and about to turn the corner when she saw something at a distance in the alley. It was old Chester with her friends, Ron and Ment. The three of them were bent over looking at something. Enid walked down the alley to get a better look. She remembered her grandmother's caution about the alley, but Ron, Ment, and Chester were there.

"What are you looking at?" she asked.

All three of them jumped at the sound of her voice.

"You scared us half to death!" Ment's voice was squeaky.

Enid looked down and saw what the three were looking at—it was a GUN! Enid moved closer. "Don't get too close," Chester warned, holding out his arm to keep her back.

"Well, what are you just staring at it for?" Enid asked.

"'Cause I told them not to touch it," Chester said. "Guns are dangerous in the wrong hands, and y'all's are the wrong hands!"

"I wonder whose gun it is?" Enid asked.

"Probably belongs to some hoodlum," Ron and Ment chimed in.

"You guess it could be from someone in the neighborhood?" Ron asked.

"Could be," Chester nodded.

"Then what are we going to do with it?" Enid was curious.

"WE won't do nothing with it. Y'all go on home, and I'll get somebody to call the police," Chester replied. "This gun could have been used to hurt or kill somebody. We have to be extra careful because it might still be loaded."

You guess it's a play gun?" Ment couldn't take his eyes off the shiny object.

"No, it's real all right," Chester's eyes rolled. "Now, y'all run home so I'll know you're not around here bothering something you got no business bothering."

"What does it feel like to be shot, Chester?" Enid asked as they all stared at the gun.

Chester couldn't believe his ears.

"Now, what kind of question is that?"

"Well, I've been wondering ever since that boy got in trouble at school today."

"It don't feel good, I can tell you that," Chester said. "Now, run along home—all of you. Go!"

So the three of them took off down the alley for home.

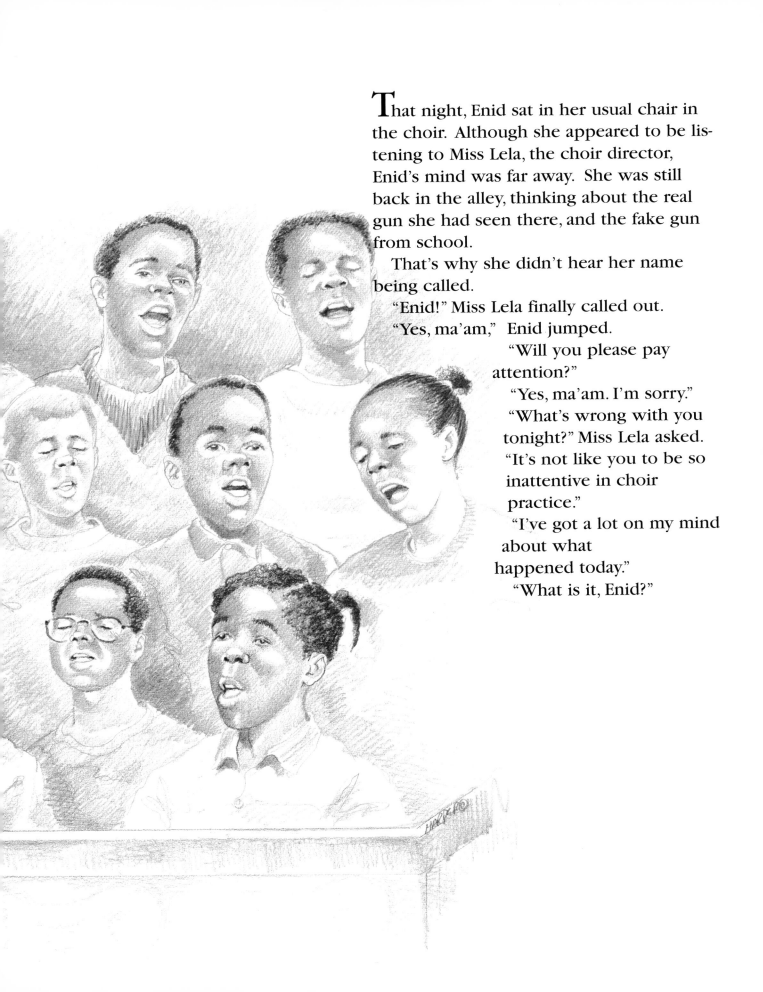

That night, Enid sat in her usual chair in the choir. Although she appeared to be listening to Miss Lela, the choir director, Enid's mind was far away. She was still back in the alley, thinking about the real gun she had seen there, and the fake gun from school.

That's why she didn't hear her name being called.

"Enid!" Miss Lela finally called out.

"Yes, ma'am," Enid jumped.

"Will you please pay attention?"

"Yes, ma'am. I'm sorry."

"What's wrong with you tonight?" Miss Lela asked. "It's not like you to be so inattentive in choir practice."

"I've got a lot on my mind about what happened today."

"What is it, Enid?"

Enid couldn't believe what came out of her mouth. But as the entire youth choir listened, Enid told the story about seeing the two guns.

When she finished, all her friends in the choir sat looking at her with wide eyes. Miss Lela just looked relieved.

"I'm glad Chester had sense enough to make you kids leave it alone. Guns are nothing to play with."

"Yes, ma'am, but I still have my question," Enid said. "I wonder what it feels like to be shot?"

"I can't tell you exactly, but I know it must hurt a great deal, Enid. When people get shot they're walking close to being killed. When we use a gun or anything else to hurt some-one, it displeases God, because he teaches us to love one another."

"I'm sure I never want to be shot!" Enid said as she sat back down. Miss Lela clapped her hands to finish rehearsal. Enid was glad she had asked her question. It was very important to her.

When Miss Lela dropped Enid off at home after practice, Grandma was sitting on the porch waiting.

"Hi, Gran," Enid said as she walked past to go into the house.

"Wait just one minute, young lady," Grandma said, "I need some sugar."

Enid smiled. She knew what that meant. Grandma wanted a kiss.

"Now, that's better," Grandma said as Enid's arms went around her neck. "You got the best sugar in the world."

Enid smiled, but was quiet.

"Is something the matter, child? Did something happen at choir practice?"

"No, Grandma—but I did tell them I saw a gun today."

"You mean the play gun that boy brought to school?"

"No! I saw a real gun."

"Where, child?" Grandma's voice rose higher.

"Back in the alley."

"You didn't touch it, did you?" Grandma's face looked worried and frightened, so Enid hurried to answer.

"No ma'am. We all saw it; Ment, Ron, and Chester. Chester called the police after we left."

"God bless old Chester," Grandma breathed a sigh of relief.

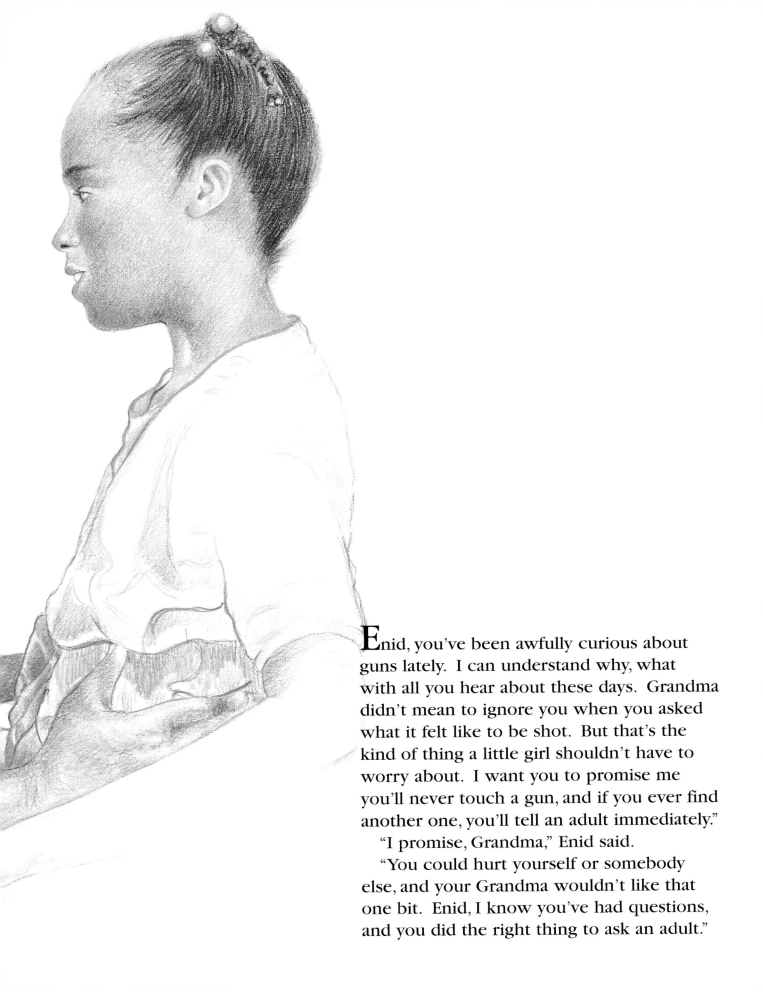

Enid, you've been awfully curious about guns lately. I can understand why, what with all you hear about these days. Grandma didn't mean to ignore you when you asked what it felt like to be shot. But that's the kind of thing a little girl shouldn't have to worry about. I want you to promise me you'll never touch a gun, and if you ever find another one, you'll tell an adult immediately."

"I promise, Grandma," Enid said.

"You could hurt yourself or somebody else, and your Grandma wouldn't like that one bit. Enid, I know you've had questions, and you did the right thing to ask an adult."

"Enid, it's bedtime. Did you brush your teeth?" her mother called. Enid ran out of the bedroom, her smile wide to show her clean teeth. The TV reporter was doing a story about the boy who was taken out of school for bringing a play gun to class. Enid heard the reporter mention something called "zero tolerance."

"What does that mean, Momma?"

"Well honey, it means folks at school won't put up with a play gun, a real gun, a knife, or any other weapon brought around our precious children. And that's a good thing."

Enid nodded her head and grinned just as her mother scooped her up in her arms and gave her a big kiss.

In the background, the reporter was talking about a meeting to discuss guns in schools. "I want to go," Enid said.

"We'll both go," her mother promised.

Reflections for Adults

The care and safety of children everywhere continues to be a growing concern.

Many things can be considered a danger to children. These include guns, drugs, discarded needles, etc.

Just as in this story of Enid, children have questions and concerns that need to be addressed by adults.

Encourage the children in your life to talk with you about their concerns.

As a parent, grandparent, teacher, guardian, or friend, you can never assume children know these simple safety guidelines.

Take the time to discuss these steps—you may save a life.

- Stop, don't touch
- Leave the area immediately
- Tell an adult, have them call the police

Added to this important lesson is one we learn from the Bible. It is simple, but timeless.

For this is the love of God, that we keep his commandments. (1 John 5:3, KJV)

Thou shalt not kill. (Exodus 20:13, KJV)